STO

3/09

FRIENDS
OF ACPL

W9-DFT-456

TATER & TOT

by ANDREA BURRIS

For my sisters, Anna and Kit who continue to inspire me.

- Andrea -

Copyright 2008 by Andrea Burris. All rights reserved. No part of this publication may be reproduced, stored in a retrieval system or transmitted, in any form, or by any means, electronic, mechanical, recorded, photocopied, or otherwise, without the prior written permission of the copyright owner, except by a reviewer who may quote brief passages in a review.

For information or orders contact :
A & D Books, 5096 E. 400, Big Cabin, OK 74332
Tel: 918-520-5862

Published by:
A & D Books, Inc.
5096 E. 400
BIg Cabin, OK 74332
Tel: 918-785-5779

Printed in China

Tater & Tot
ISBN: 978-0-9743294-2-0   US $15.95   CANADA $20.95

Tater and Tot were brothers.

Wherever Tater went, Tot followed.

Sometimes, trouble followed too...

While it's true that Tater and Tot love potatoes, really, they were just trying to help Mrs. Simpkins carry her groceries across the street.

"They're taking my groceries!" she yelled.

"WOOF! WOOF!" squealed Tater and Tot which, of course, meant "NO! NO!"

The policeman blew his whistle loudly. Tires squealed! Horns blew! Eggs and milk,potatoes and fruit all flew into the air as the bags went UP,

and Mrs. Simpkins went DOWN.
Such confusion! Could Tater and Tot really be held responsible for this huge mess?!

Perhaps so . . . . .

So it was that Tater and Tot came to be at the Hillsdale Animal Shelter.

Tater and Tot watched the door and waited.

"This is another fine mess you've gotten us into" sobbed Tot, but Tater was not worried.

"Nonsense! Someone will come to take us home, a home of our very own! I sure hope they like potatoes as much as we do." Tater was dreaming and drooling.

They stared at the door, watching. Now . . . . .ok, NOW . . . . .still they watched and waited . . . . maybe . . . . NOW! Just as their hope started to waiver, the doorknob slowly turned.

A small curly-haired boy named Stuart came in. He wanted a dog so badly! And when Tater and Tot saw Stuart, they just knew he was there to rescue them. They jumped, barked, and made such a noise! They wagged and yipped as he opened the cage and jumped into his arms. Stuart knew these were the dogs he was hoping to find.

As they walked home, Stuart said: "I sure hope Mom and Dad will let me keep you." Tater and Tot were not concerned. "How could Stuart's parents not want to keep them?!" "Woof!" said Tater, which of course meant "Nonsense!"

Tater and Tot waited outside while Stuart went in to talk to his parents. They could hear parts of the conversation. . . . ."oh, PLEEEAAASSSEEE". . . . . and, "no dog right now". . . . . . . and, "MOVING?!"

Tot looked at Tater and said, "I think that could have gone better."
Tater wailed, "I don't think it could have gone any worse!"

Stuart came out with tears in his eyes. "They said we're moving and that I can't have a dog right now." The three of them sat there. . . . . . . stewing.

Tater and Tot went from glum to hopeful as Stuart stood up and declared resolutely, "I'll sneak you onto the moving truck! If you move with us, they'll have to let me keep you!"

Tater and Tot hid in the back yard until moving day. The truck was almost loaded. Stuart took an empty box to the back yard. He wrote "Stuart's Room" on the outside. After punching holes in the box, Tater and Tot jumped in and he taped it closed. Stuart had a problem! With both dogs in the box, he couldn't lift it. He asked one of the moving men for help. "No problem," he said. I'll take care of it." The moving man went inside the house and got the last few boxes. He never found the box in the back yard. He went back out and closed up the truck. Stuart's mom made a last check of the house while Stuart and his dad waited in the car. She turned off the last light, locked the door and joined them. Tater and Tot looked at each other in horror as they heard the truck and the family car drive away. "OH NO!" they cried. "DON'T LEAVE US!" They barked and jumped until the box flew open. They chased after the truck and car, but it was too late. They were gone!

Exhausted, they went back to the house and stared at it sadly. "We almost had a home" said Tater. "Yes, I know" said Tot.

"I'll bet they liked potatoes as much as we do" said Tater. "Probably" said Tot.

They looked at the moving box again. There was the new address on the box to where Stuart and his family were moving. "OUR family!" cried Tot. "We must find them!"

Tater looked at the address again. "Is that very far away, Tot?"

"Yes, I'm afraid so. We'll have to go downtown to the train station."

They walked for miles. When they reached downtown, they stopped just outside a restaurant.

"I am SO HUNGRY!" said Tater

"I don't think we should be here" said Tot. The sign outside says "Coat and Tie Required".

"The sign doesn't say "NO DOGS," said Tater. "We just need a coat and tie."

"I still don't think this is a good idea," said Tot.

"Nonsense!" said Tater.

Borrowing two coats and ties from the coatroom, Tater and Tot went in wearing their less-than-perfect-fitting clothes. The hostess looked down, stared, started to say something, then shrugged her shoulders and said "Right this way, please."

The waiter came, stared, and then after a long pause said, "What will you have, sir?"

"Woof!" said Tater, pointing to the menu.

"Excellent choice" said the waiter. "And you, sir?"

"Rrrrrrrrr, woof!" said Tot.

"Very good" said the waiter and left.

The meal was wonderful, but oh, the MASHED PO-TATOES, BAKED POTATOES and FRENCH FRIES!

"Yummylisish!" said Tater. He was drooling again. Tot agreed.

Everything was great until the bill came. Horrified, Tot whispered to Tater. "The sign didn't say we needed money!"

The waiter scowled.

3 1833 05663 7728

Fortunately, Tater and Tot knew just how to clean dishes.

Tater and Tot finally made it to the train station. They waited until the conductor went by and jumped onto the train. The train car they picked had beds in it, perfect for two tired dogs.

"Maybe we shouldn't" said Tot.

"Nonsense!" said Tater.

Tater climbed up into the berth. Tot was about to follow him when he saw a lady coming. He hid. She climbed into the same berth as Tater. After a moment there was horrible screaming and a great commotion as she jumped out and ran down the aisle.

Tater stuck his head out. "What's the matter with her?" he asked. Tot stared after the lady and shook his head.

"Let's find somewhere else to sleep on the train" he whispered. "We don't want to get kicked off!"

Tater and Tot made new friends in the baggage car.

They forgot all about being tired.

They traveled all night and the next day, too. When the train finally came into the station, they were very tired and very hungry.

Tot said, "We'll have to take a bus to the next town, but they may not let dogs on the bus."

"No problem," said Tater.

"What does THAT mean?" asked Tot.

Tater went into a nearby shop and came out with shirts, hats and sunglasses.

"Now we can get on the bus" he said triumphantly.

Tater and Tot followed the other people onto the bus.
"I am SO HUNGRY" whispered Tater.
"Try not to think about it" said Tot, but that was all Tater
could think about. And then he noticed that the lady in
front of them had POTATO CHIPS in her shopping bag.
"Yummylishish" whispered Tater. He was drooling
again.
"I don't think you should" said Tot.
"Nonsense!" said Tater. He just couldn't resist.
Those chips were soooooooooo tasty!
     Tater was licking every potato-chippy-paw when Tot
said "I think we're almost there."

It was a long bus ride, but they finally came to the town where Stuart and his family lived. It seemed like such a BIG city.

"How will we get there now?" asked Tot.

"Follow me" said Tater.

As they walked through the parking lot, Tater stopped next to a motorcycle with a sidecar.

"OH NO! We shouldn't!" said Tot.

"Nonsense!" said Tater. "You drive!"

Tot started the motorcycle reluctantly as Tater wedged himself into the sidecar. They zoomed down the street. They were so close now. They stopped at a traffic light. Just as the light was ready to change, a man driving a panel truck pulled up next to them. Tot looked at his truck. It read "City Dog Catcher" in large blue letters on the side. They looked at each other.

"Hey, you!" he yelled as the light changed.

Tot took off with the dog catcher right behind him. Miles and miles they went. Finally stopped by a traffic light, the dog catcher jumped out and threw his net over Tater. Tot could have escaped, but he would not leave Tater behind.

"This is the worst!" wailed Tater.

"I know" said Tot.

But they were not the only ones who were sad. Stuart's parents were concerned. Stuart had been very sad ever since they had arrived the week before. "Let's go for a drive" his dad suggested.

Stuart rode in the back seat and said nothing. He didn't care where they were going. When they got there, he followed behind, not noticing or caring. As his father opened the door, he asked Stuart, "How would you like a dog, son?"

Stuart found it hard to look at all of the dogs, but he walked
down the aisle. He stopped and stared. Stuart saw Tater
and Tot in their cage   and they saw him. They
wagged and yipped   as he opened the
cage and jumped   into his arms.

"Tater and Tot" he exclaimed!
His dad smiled, "I guess they were in the right place at the
right time!" Let's go home!